The Cafeteria Lady
from the
Black Lagoon

by Mike Thaler · pictures by Jared Lee

SCHOLASTIC INC.

New York Toronto London Auckland Sydney

For Jo Small, my sister,
with love
—M.T.

To Spanky and Little Din
—J.L.

Library of Congress Catalog Card Number: 97-61899
ISBN 0-590-50493-2
Text copyright © 1998 by Mike Thaler.
Illustrations copyright © 1998 by Jared D. Lee Studio, Inc.
All rights reserved. Published by Scholastic Inc.
10 9 8 7 6 5 4 3 2 1   8 9/9 0/0 01 02
Printed in the U.S.A.   24
First printing, September 1998

We got a new cafeteria lady today.
Her name is Wanda Belch.

Eric says that instead of a car, she drives
a garbage truck to school.

Freddy heard that she learned to cook on a pirate ship, so don't go near the kitchen.

Derek says that at Wanda's old school, kids found sneakers and baseball caps in her tuna surprise.

And when class pets disappeared . . .

The kids made sure to check the specials the next day.

All the kids say that Wanda uses natural ingredients in her dishes: organic rats in her *ratatouille*...

sweaty socks in her *moussaka*...

gooey ghouls in her *goulash*...

real sand and witches in her sandwiches.

We've heard Wanda's into recycling.
The water she washes the dishes in will be . . .

tomorrow's soup of the day.

I heard she doesn't throw *anything* away!

I wonder what Wanda's cooking up right now?
Today's menu will probably be:

ROADKILL RAVIOLI

SPAGHETTI WITH BOWLING BALLS

SOUFFLÉ OF SCIENCE EXPERIMENTS
and TOXIC WASTE TACOS

For dessert we might have ton cake,
which is pound cake . . .

only heavier.

Even if you can't eat the food, they say
it's always good for something.
The meatballs are aerodynamic...

the mashed potatoes are good for sculpting...

the pudding will stick to anything...

and the spinach is great for vinyl repairs.

I hope the spaghetti will make good shoelaces.

Uh-oh, it's time for lunch!
I'm too young to die.
Can't we have a math test instead?
Isn't it time for vaccinations?

We're being lined up and marched down to the *cafetorium*.

I'll bet Wanda's stirring up poisonous pots
full of molten messes of steamy slime.

We're through the door.
We get our trays.
They don't even offer us blindfolds.

Hey! Wanda doesn't look so bad.
And look! She made hamburgers and french fries.

They smell good if you take your hand off your nose.
I'm going to get two!

Gobble, gobble, munch, munch.
Look out, stomach, here comes lunch!
Hey, these taste great!
Maybe I'll get three more.

There are even homemade chocolate-chip cookies for dessert!
Lunchtime is going to be my favorite class.

Maybe Wanda will let us stay for dinner?